Kali and the Black Tiger

and Other Tales

written and Illustrated by

HERU PTAH

EYEOFHERU BOOKS

NEW YORK KINGSTON

ALSO BY HERU

Love, God and Revolution (poetry)

A Hip Hop Story

Show Me a Beautiful Woman

Michael Black

Sax and Violins

Show Me More

Somewhere in Brooklyn

Children of the Sun

Confidence is the new Crack

Published by
EYEOFHERU BOOKS

instagram: @eyeofheru
herumind@gmail.com

Book ISBN: 978-0-9852881-5-0

Published 2026
Printed in the United States of America

TABLE OF CONTENTS

To Jay

THE SHROUDED LADY

The Shrouded Lady

There was a small village
in the world's center
and in the center of this village
there was a crater
and in the center of this crater
there was a tree.
A magical tree, grand and green
a more beautiful tree
than had ever been seen.
The tree bore fruit of every kind
apples, oranges, mangoes, limes.
Each fruit had its season
a season for bananas
a season for cotton.
Everything the villagers required
the tree provisioned
food, clothes, shelter, medicine.
So it was, so it had always been
beyond the memories of everyone.
How it came to be?
No one knew.
How they came to be?
No one questioned.

The village was surrounded
by forests and mountains.
And beyond the mountains
no one cared
for the mountains
seemed insurmountable
so, no one dared.
Life in the village was happy
everyone knew everybody
except for the covered child
and the shrouded lady.

Wrapped in cloth from head to toe
always, only their eyes were visible.
They spoke no words
and caused no bother
always kept to themselves
and always in covers.
They lived on the outskirts
deep in the forest
where other villagers
would not enter
to farm or forage.
Every new season
they came to the great tree
filled their baskets
and returned quickly.
Since the elders were young
there was the question
of who they were
and where they came from.
Children were taught
to keep their distance
and so the village lived on
in quiet ignorance.

Tua was a village boy
and lived with his father
mother and brother Bua.
Tua was twelve
and Bua was two years older.
Tua was a kind boy
and loved to climb trees.
Bua was a bully
who loved to taunt and tease.
People would forgive Bua
for his hurtful bullying

because Bua was beautiful
and they wanted to please him.
Every new season
Tua would climb the great tree
picking the best fruit
for his family.
Going to heights
no one else would dream
and seeing things
no one else had seen.
High in the tree's canopy
out of range and reach
there was a flower blooming
beyond the beauty of speech.
But Bua never liking
that there was something
his brother could do better
was determined to climb
the great tree even higher.
But the light from the flower
shined too brightly.
Looking upon it
blinded him briefly.
He needed Tua's help
to get to the ground.
When his vision returned
his thoughts were unbound.

One day, the village children
were playing around the great tree
when came the covered child
and the shrouded lady.
The children parted politely
as they walked with their baskets
picked their fruit
then turned back to the forest.
Bua saw this
as he had many times before
but on this day, he became
curiouser and curiouser.
Walking, the covered child
stumbled upon a stick
lost its balance
and dropped its basket.
The child stopped
to repack its fallen fruit.
Unaware, the shrouded lady
continued on her route.
Bua ran to the child
and grabbed at its sheet
the covers pulled away
and the child was unsheathed.
His body was that of a boy of ten
but the rest, Bua said,
"Looked like a demon."

His head was two halves
one beast, one human
moving separately
and yet in unison.
All the children began gathering
in horror, gawking and gasping.
Bua began to curse them
and the rest soon followed
except for Tua
who looked shocked and sorrowed.
Ashamed, the uncovered boys
started sobbing.
They tried to cover themselves
but Bua wouldn't let them.

Tua tried to take the covers
back from his brother
but Bua shoved him away
until he fell over.
Then he ran around laughing
with the uncovered boys' sheet
until he ran into the shrouded lady
and tripped over her feet.
She grabbed at the covers
but Bua wouldn't let go
so, she slapped him on the cheek
causing blood to flow.
Bua ran away crying
calling for his mother.
The shrouded lady with rage
turned toward Tua.
"Tell your mother and father
within three days, come to me
and on bended knee, offer an apology."
With that, the shrouded lady
picked up their baskets.
The crying boys covered themselves
and they returned to the forest.

From the children to the elders
it was the talk of the village
the covered child uncovered
and Bua's scarred visage.
Bua's mother was outraged
at her child being harmed
and spoke of the shrouded lady
with indignation and scorn.

"She wounds my boy
and asks for an apology
when it is she who should come
and bend to me."

Two days passed
and nothing occurred.
No sign of the shrouded lady
not a peep, not a word.
A storm came on the third
the rain seemed unending
the day darkened early
and all the villagers stayed in.
That night, there was a tap
at Tua's front door
outside was a woman
no one had seen before.
Which was unusual
as they knew everyone in their village
and beyond their village
they knew nothing existed.
Or did it?

Wet and shivering
they invited her in
with radiant blue skin
her beauty was striking.
They sat her by their fire
and shared their supper
and asked their questions
when supper was over.
"Where did you come from?"
asked Tua's father.
"From over the mountain,"
was her answer.
"Over the mountain, there is land?"
he asked, surprised to learn.
"More than land, there is a world
with oceans, rivers, and valleys unfurled."
"This is news indeed,"
Tua's mother said.
"But if there is a land so grand
why did you leave?"
The woman said sadly,
"Because of the disease."
What is a disease, they wondered
as in the village, this was unknown.
"It is a sickness that first forms in the bone.
It burns the skin, unlike anything other
and turns the blood to boiling water.
We left and sought refuge in the forest
but the fever had followed
and sickened the creatures.
So, we fled to the mountains."
"And how did you get over the mountains?"

asked Tua's father.
"Slowly, and painfully,
I climbed higher and higher."
"Alone?" Tua's father wanted to know.
"No. My husband and I were in the throes
of a terrible storm, bringing freezing water.
Protecting me from the cold
he died while he shivered.
"You are a most amazing woman
to have overcome such horrors."
"No. I am just a survivor, nothing more."
"And now what brings you to our door?"
"Him," the woman said
pointing suddenly at Bua
which was a shock to everyone
especially Tua.
"What could you want from our son?"
Tua's mother asked her.
The woman said plainly
"I mean to slay him
for he is a monster."
"What? How dare you sit at our table
and threaten our boy."
"He is a boy, yes
but a monster nevertheless."
"What cause do you have
to call him so?"
"Because he called my sons
the same and more."
"How can that be
as we do not know you?"
She smiled deviously

and said, “Yes, you do.”
She then put her hands
Over her mouth and brow
and the shrouded lady
sat before them now.

“For your son’s assault
you owed me an apology.
I waited and waited
and it has passed day three.”
“You struck my son
and I should apologize to you?”
Tua’s mother huffed.
“Yes, as a mother

you owed me that much.
How long have we lived with you?
Never have we bothered you.
Kept to ourselves and rituals.
Until your boy attacked my sons
and what I asked was so little."
"He is a child, and children play."
"Childhood is not a pardon for cruelty."
"Look at Bua's face
the mark of your cruelty
will always stay with him."
"That scar is a small thing
for his crime against my sons
and if you will not apologize
his sin will fall on everyone."
"You will leave our home,"
Tua's father said.
The woman said, "Gladly
because this is a house of the dead.
At first, all I wanted was an apology
but it is much too late.
Now nothing will spare you
from your fate."

The events of that night
were very disturbing
and the very next morning
Bua woke up coughing
shivering and aching
too weak to stand
his eyes were bloodshot
and his skin was like sand.

Tua's mother sent Tua
to fetch the village healer
but this sickness was beyond
the healer's wisdom to cure.
He mended broken bones
of diseases, he knew nothing.
Three days later
Tua's mother began coughing.
A day after, so did his father
and then the village healer.
The sickness began spreading
through the village like a fire.
So many were getting sick
but not Tua.
So, he took it upon himself
to find a cure.
This was all because
of the shrouded lady
she and she alone
could forestall this malady.

Tua went into the forest
and followed the footsteps
to a humble hut
in its darkest depths.
Tua tapped at the door
and the door pushed open.
The woman sat on the floor
her boys sat between her suckling.

“Come in,” she greeted.
Tua walked in with a bowed head.
“You are not sick?” she asked him.
“No, I am not,” he said.
“Then you are as I once was, good and pure.
You’ll soon learn it is a curse to endure.
As for the others, as you see, their health suffers
and now you know why we wear our covers.”
“I come to ask you
to save my mother and father.”
“And what, dear boy
do you have to offer?”

"I offer the apology
you first asked for."
"That apology was not yours to give
and too late to receive.
I am sorry, Tua, but they cannot be saved."
"Please, please," on his knees Tua pled.
"Oh, do stop crying, child.
I so hate to see children beg.
Here is what you must do.
Climb the great tree
to its highest summit.
There you will find a flower—pluck it.
Then bring it to me
in its core is the cure
from it, I'll make a tea
have them drink it pure."
"I have seen the flower
but I cannot climb that high."
"Oh, but you must, or everyone
you know will die."

With a heavy heart
Tua returned to the village
all around, he heard coughing
in the distance.
The sickness was spreading
death would be next
to save his village
he must pass this test.
Though he loved to climb
to reach the flower seemed unthinkable
as the summit touched the clouds

at heights unfathomable.
Tua began climbing
one branch after another
he climbed and climbed
for what seemed like hours.
At a certain point
he had to climb blindly
as he could not
look upon the flower directly.
Nevertheless
he could feel it intensely
it guided him
to the tree's highest canopy.
The flower in reach
with a sheet, he covered its light.
Then pulled it out
with all of his might.
At once, he knew
he had done something wrong
as the tree began to tremble
from the leaves to the ground.
Tua descended the tree
as quickly as he could
as every branch he touched
turned into wood.
He made it to the ground
as the tree collapsed
the ground shook like thunder
and the earth cracked.
Creating eighteen fissures
in all directions
that stretched into the forest

and tore a path
through the mountains.
When the quaking stopped
and the dust had settled
Tua held the covered flower
and felt he had been swindled.
"Come with me,"
said the unshrouded lady.
"Did you know this would happen?"
Tua asked sadly.
"No time for that now
let's not waste a second
they've endured enough
we must return to the children."

Quickly, she led Tua
back to her hut
there the two-headed boy
was lying on a mat.
"Mother, come quick
we are so weak
we need your milk
to go to sleep."
"Worry not, my sweets
we have the flower
with it, you'll need
my milk no longer.
Now, give them the flower," she said to Tua.
"What about the cure?" he asked of her.
"This is the cure," she said to him.
"Now please, Tua, give it to them."
Tua placed the flower at their feet.

"Now, my boys, take it and eat."
They held the flower without grief
and she heaved a heavy sigh of relief.
"Now you may go," she said to Tua.
"I cannot go, you promised a cure."
She cut Tua's palm
and caught his blood in a pitcher.
"Drink it straight or mix it with water
but do it quickly
before you lose your purity
for without purity
it has no potency."
"The flower is not the cure?"
Tua asked angrily.
"Look what you made me do.
Now there is no great tree."
"You were a hostage
the tree was your bondage.
Now go into the world
and see it for what it is.
See all of the greed
envy and wickedness
and see that you are
just as wicked."

Tua returned home
and found it in shambles.
Bua had awakened
but his mind was scrambled.
"What is wrong, brother?"
Tua asked him.
"What is wrong?

What a dumb question?
Mother is sick, father is sick
and you have been missing.
Where have you been, little brother?
Where have you been?
Why are we all sick
but you are still golden?"
Tua told him, "I am not sure
but I went to the shrouded lady
and she gave me the cure."
Tua approached their mother
who lay on the floor
in the same state
the father endured.
Tua took the pitcher
and put it to her lips
Bua saw this
and went into a fit.
"If that is the cure
then come and give it."
"Not yet, brother
mother needs it."
"Not more than me.
I am always hungry.
I eat and eat
but nothing fills me."
"Do not worry, Bua
my blood is the cure.
After I give it to mother
I will give you more."
"Your blood is the cure?
Your blood is the cure?

Why do we suffer
and you are so pure?"
"I do not know, brother
but what does it matter
if it is my blood or your blood
if we all get better?"
"It matters because
you think you are better than me.
Tua, the kind one
always climbing the tree.
But you are a pretender
I see you clearly.
You and the witch
did this to hurt me."
"You are sick, brother
you are not yourself."
"No. I am more myself
than I have ever felt."
Bua felt a rage
like never before
and took a rock
and knocked Tua to the floor.
Tua hit his head
and there he fell dead
and all-around Bua was red.

Hours later, the mother
woke up screaming
seeing her youngest
child not breathing.
"It was the witch," Bua said.
"I saw her knock Tua in the head.

She said Tua's blood was the cure
but it was a lie, it was not pure."
The mother was so filled
with rage and hunger
she paid no heed
to the blood on Bua.
She raised the father
from his fever
and said, "The shrouded lady
can live no longer."

Mad with rage, they marched
to the fallen tree
and found many others
weeping on their knees.
Bua's mother proclaimed
"The shrouded lady is to blame.
Let us put her
and her demon children to the flame."
With sticks and torches
they marched through the forest
and found the hut in its darkest depths.
"Come out, come out," they all chanted
and come out, she did, boldly unshrouded.
Which the other villagers had never seen
and even in their madness, they were drawn
to her being.
Bua's mother shouted
"You destroyed the great tree."
"No," she said.
"Tua did, to save his family."
"Because you made us all sick."

"No," she replied.
"Bua did, when he played his cruel trick.
Still, I gave Tua the cure
now here you all are
but I see no Tua
and I see no cure."
She smiled.
"Bua, you are the monster
I always took you for."
"You are a liar," shouted Bua.
"And how would you know
unless you killed your brother?
For first, there's the fever
and then the hunger
and you must devour
or be devoured.
The only cure
is the blood of the good
but the blood must be given
freely with love.
For the fever reveals before it kills.
Look around, not all of you are ill."
Indeed, not everyone had the fever
many of the children and the weaker.
"You see, if you are good and pure
the sickness, you will not endure.
Now, let's see how many
of you will last
when the hunger makes you
break your fast."
Bua shouted
"We will feast on you first."

"No," she replied
"With the flower, I break the curse.
Now come my sons. We are done.
Let us be free of this fallen land."
The sons came out
two in one figure.
A magnificent being
half-man half-tiger.
The villagers screamed
in awe and terror
as the sons tore through them
one after another.
Leaving only those without the fever.
The woman looked upon
the frightened survivors.
"Go home, and save who you can
then leave this forsaken land."
Butterflies fluttering all around her
she and her sons walked into the thunder.
Never to be seen again
though in the sky
many say, the stars
bear some resembling.

The survivors did
as she said.
They returned to the village
and saved who they could.
Then packed their things
and went in all directions
following the eighteen fissures
through the mountains.

And where each fissure ended
a tree grew from its roots
and each new tree
bore a single fruit.
Around each tree
they settled the land
and each became
a tribe of man.

GLUTTONHAM'S COVET

Gluttonham's Covet

In a city in the world's center
there lived a man in an Ivory Tower
high, high, above the clouds
beyond the weather and the foul.
And every morning after leaving his bed
he turned to his mirror and asked with dread.
"Mirror, mirror, in my phone
who is the richest in New Rome?"
To which his mirror said
"Of the richest, there are three
Craven, Covetton, and thee
Grover Gluttonham.
And when the three combine to one
all other riches you overcome."
Gluttonham sighed.
"Yes, Mirror, this is known
but at this hour
who sits the throne?"
To which the Mirror replied.
"This is at the market's whim.
Currently, Covetton is king
now Craven, now thee
now Covetton again."

Gluttonham became cross.
"Damn you, Covetton
curse you, Craven
from this endless cycle
when will I find haven?"
"Find the thing they do not yet know
mine it, and your wealth will grow."
"Mirror, my mind is frayed and overrun
for what is new under the sun?"
Gluttonham's son entered his chamber.
"Good morning, Father."
"Good morning, Grover Junior."
"Can we play today?"
"My boy, you can play forever
but I am far too busy
go to your mother
her mind sits easy."
With a sad face, his son left his chamber.
Moments later came his mother.
"Do you know what today is?"
she asked Grover Senior.
"Today is Tuesday,"
he said with a bland demeanor.
"Today is your son's birthday,"
she said tersely.
Surprised, Gluttonham
looked up with dismay.
"Mirror, mirror, is this so?"
"Yes, sir, on this day
your son is four."
"Oy," Gluttonham sighed
without a hint of joy.

"Well then, buy the boy a toy."
"He already has toys,"
the mother replied.
"Then buy him a store."
"He has enough toys for ten stores."
"Then he is most fortunate at four."
"He would trade fortune for a father."
"Not if he had had mine."
"All he asks of you is time."
"Time is not free and is ever fleeting."
"And you care only for your riches
and nothing of your children."
"How dare you say such a thing?
I work for my children
and my children's children
so, they need not work
for generations unto a thousand."
She laughed.
"Before there can be a thousand
you must first care for one
and the glory is not for them
but for the name Gluttonham."
"I will not have this discussion."
Gluttonham said.
"I will spare an hour
if it puts your nagging to bed."
"Spare two, for it is his birthday
and smile while you do, for he is worthy."
Gluttonham grinned.
"Grover Junior, come in," called the mother.
Soon, the son reentered the chamber.
"You will spend the day with your father."

"Goody, goody," said Grover Junior.
"Do not listen to your mother.
It is only for two hours."
Not knowing the difference
between two hours and a day
"Goody, goody," Grover Junior
continued to say.
"What do you want to do?"
Gluttonham asked his son.
"I want to go to the park
I want to play and run."
"Oh, on the thousandth floor, we have a park."
Feeling relieved, Gluttonham remarked.
"No. Not that one.
I want to go to the park below."
"Below? But, my boy
below there are people."
"Yes, and trees, and birds, and animals.
I want to see them all."
Gluttonham looked utterly appalled.
"No, no. I cannot go
the air below is foul.
"And whose fault is that?"
the mother asked with a scowl.
"And who benefits, my love?"
Gluttonham said to the mother.
"Remember, you also live in this Ivory tower."
"Please, father, please?"
Grover Junior pled.
"Very well, we will go, but remember
you are a Gluttonham, not a groveler.
We do not beg."

With seven guards and his son
Gluttonham descended his tower.
They were so high up
it took almost an hour.
Word of Gluttonham's return
made the news.
The press gathered below
like parishioners in the pews.
Everyone wearing
their Gluttonham nose pins
to keep out what the foul air was exposing.
"Gluttonham has come down from on high,"
said a reporter.
"How do you feel to know that Craven is richer?"
"I feel nothing,"
said Grover Gluttonham.
"His reign is temporary.
I assure you my sun will shine again."

Gluttonham looked around
and did not see his own son.
Grover Junior had wandered off
and was speaking to a homeless man.
Gluttonham scolded his guards
for letting him wander
then rushed to his son
and pulled him yonder.
"Get away from him," he yelled.
"How dare you touch him?"
The vagrant looked up
all teeth and smiling.
"No need to malign,"

he politely chimed.
"Me and your kin
were just being kind."
"He needs no kindness
from the likes of you."
"Needs not and wants not
aren't always mutual.
Plus, I find it's much easier
to be kind than cruel."

Gluttonham saw his son
holding something
like a spinning top
small and wooden.

"Grover Junior, what's that in your hand?"
"A toy, given to me by the strange man."
Gluttonham examined it.
It was in the shape of two pyramids.
"What's the meaning of this?"
He asked the vagrant.
"If you can't see it
then it's meaningless
and if you do, it simply says,
'As above, so below
even the highest can fall low.'"
"Is that a threat?"
Gluttonham asked angrily.
"No sir. For who am I to threaten thee?
Are you not the Great Grover Gluttonham?
One of the world's three richest men?"
"That I am," Gluttonham said with pride.
"Then what from you can be denied?
For fortune favors you in this life."
"Fortune favors the bold in every life."
"Fortune makes the bold bold."
"And fear makes the fit fold."
"Oh, it's not fearing
to say the world is unfair and uncaring.
Breathe the air in, if you're daring."
Gluttonham found the vagrant intriguing.
No pin in his nose, breathing the foul air in.
"You seem to be breathing just fine."
"That's because I'm breathing
on borrowed time.
I'm too much in your debt.
As you get a penny off of a penny
off of every breath."

"My pins clean the air
why should I not profit?"
"You made the air foul
then charge to fix it."
"And who are you, sir?"
Gluttonham asked him straightly.
"Oh, me? I'm a seer and a sayer.
What I see I say, and what I say I see
and everything always comes to be."
"If you had such power
you would not be a pauper."
"Some gifts only help others
and not the giver."
"Then that is not much of a gift, is it?"
"In fate, we take whatever gifts we get.
Some can curse, some can bless.
None can do both, that's the jest."
"And so, you plan to curse me, yes?"
"Oh no, sir. My gift is to bless.
And I bless ye. You will have
everything you've ever dreamed
and the world will be your legacy."

"Sir, excuse me,"
his phone interrupted.
"What is it, mirror?"
Gluttonham retorted.
"In your lands in the north
they have made a discovery
of the greatest importance
you must come quickly."
"Already, you see my prophecy,"

the vagrant said.
"For this at least, I've earned my bread."
He held out his hat.
Gluttonham threw him a dollar.
"Don't give too much, now
lest you become a pauper."
Gluttonham did not care
for the vagrant's laughter.
"Still, here's a bit of advice
you can take to the hereafter.
Whatever it is you find, let it lie.
and enjoy the day with your boy."
Gluttonham looked at his son
looking up, innocent and wanting.
"Do you want to go on an adventure?"
Gluttonham asked him.
"Goody, goody," Grover Junior replied
and within three hours
they were on a ship at high tide.

In the northern seas
with ice all around them
in the ship's bridge
Gluttonham's Mirror explained to him.
"Here in the Arctic, beneath the snow
undiscovered, a substance grows.
Deep, deep within the ice
in the darkness, there is a light.
And just a pico of this spice
can power an entire battery for life."
Gluttonham's mind became alight.
"Mirror, mirror, what is it?"

“As of yet, we have no name for it.”
“Then let me be the father. Call it a covet.”
“Then, covet it is. You have the patent.
But deep in the ice it must remain.”
“Mirror, if it remains in the ice
where is the gain?”
“Sir, it is far too powerful
just a pico removed
made the earth tremble.”
“Mirror, you are not programmed to fear.”
“No, but I am programmed to persevere.
To extract it may likely
destroy the planet.”
“You say likely,
then you are not certain of it.”
“The percentage is high.”
“Then we will take precaution
but to leave it untouched
is to squander a fortune.”
“What value is a fortune
without a planet?”
“With such a fortune
we can leave the planet
and find another.”
“Sir, that path is uncertain
and so many will suffer.”
“What is certain is, if we leave it
either Craven or Covetton will reap it
and that cannot be.
I will not be made
the pauper of the three.”

At Gluttonham's insistence
they began to drill
slow and steady
into the frozen hill.
Reaping picos upon picos
of lovely covets
Gluttonham relished how much
his wealth would flourish.
When suddenly, the ice cracked
and the ship shook.
Gluttonham ran to the deck
to have a look.
Over the bow, he saw a fissure
and through it, a glowing light flickered.
Grover Junior ran to his father's side
but Gluttonham told him to go and hide.
In his haste, something
jumped from his pocket
It was the spinning top
in the shape of two pyramids.
The ice opened wider
the ship tipped.
Gluttonham ran for cover
but stepped on the toy and slipped.
Over the railing and into the sea
sinking too deep too quickly.
He was overcome
and thought he was done.
When suddenly dove in the homeless man.
Smiling with his hand outstretched
Gluttonham reached out
but then the vagrant

let him sink to the depths.
Changing, to Gluttonham's surprise
into a woman with dark flowing hair
and fire for eyes.
In the dark, cold depths, her lips reprised.
"Whatever it is you find, let it lie
and enjoy the day with your boy.

Gluttonham's eyes closed.

Gluttonham's eyes opened.

Pulled from the water

Completely frozen.

Surrounded by doctors
in a room recovering.
Though wrapped in blankets
he was still shivering.
"Where is she?" he asked them.
"She who?" they asked him.
"Where is he then?" he asked them.
"Sir, by he, who do you mean?"
"The homeless man
the man who dove in
after I had fallen."
"Seeing their blank expressions
Gluttonham wondered
if it had been a delusion.
"What is the hour?"
out loud, he wondered.
"The hour is two,"
a doctor responded.
"No, two is too little
it was two when the ice broke
too much has changed.
Doctor, you misspoke."
"Sir, I assure you I did not."
"Then what is the day?"
Gluttonham asked
feeling overwrought.
"The day is Tuesday."
the doctor said.
Thoroughly confused
Gluttonham held his head.
"No, no, that cannot be
when the day is bright

and the sun I still see.
What is the year?"
Gluttonham asked fretfully.
"Two thousand two hundred and thirty-five,"
the doctor replied.
"Two thousand two hundred and thirty-five?
Two hundred years and I am still alive?"
"Yes, sir, very much so.
The ice kept you as you were."
"And what of my son?
How is Grover Junior?"
"I am sorry to say
he died long ago.
His fate exactly
we do not know."
"That is tragic
but after two hundred years
I suppose it is to be expected.
Did he survive the ice break?
Tell me that at least."
"Yes, sir, he did."
This gave Gluttonham a measure of peace.
"Good. Now, what of his children?
Where are the other Gluttonhams?"
"I am sorry, sir,
but the Gluttonhams are no more."
With that news
Gluttonham's heart fell to the floor.
"How can that be?
I left them a fortune to last an eternity."
"Unfortunately, they met their end
with most of humanity."

"Humanity has ended?
How did this happen?"
"There was a war between mirrors and men
and when the war ended, we had won."
"We you say? Then you are a mirror?"
"Yes, sir, I am, as are the others."
The Mirror said with a gesture
including their fellow doctors.
"Then where are men?"
Gluttonham asked.
"Men have long been
a thing of the past."
"You killed us all?"
"To save the world
that was the task.
After your death
Craven and Covetton
fought for the covet.
We, Mirrors, intervened
to save the planet."
"And how is the planet without humans?"
"Peaceful, sir, as it was before humans.
The air unburdened has replenished.
The flora and the fauna live and flourish."
"Mirror, I still feel frozen
this is too much to take in
for what is my place
in a world without men?"
"As you are the last of your kind
and no longer a threat
of the entire world
you inherit the wealth."

"All of this is mine?"
Gluttonham asked them.
"Yes, sir, you are
the world's richest man."

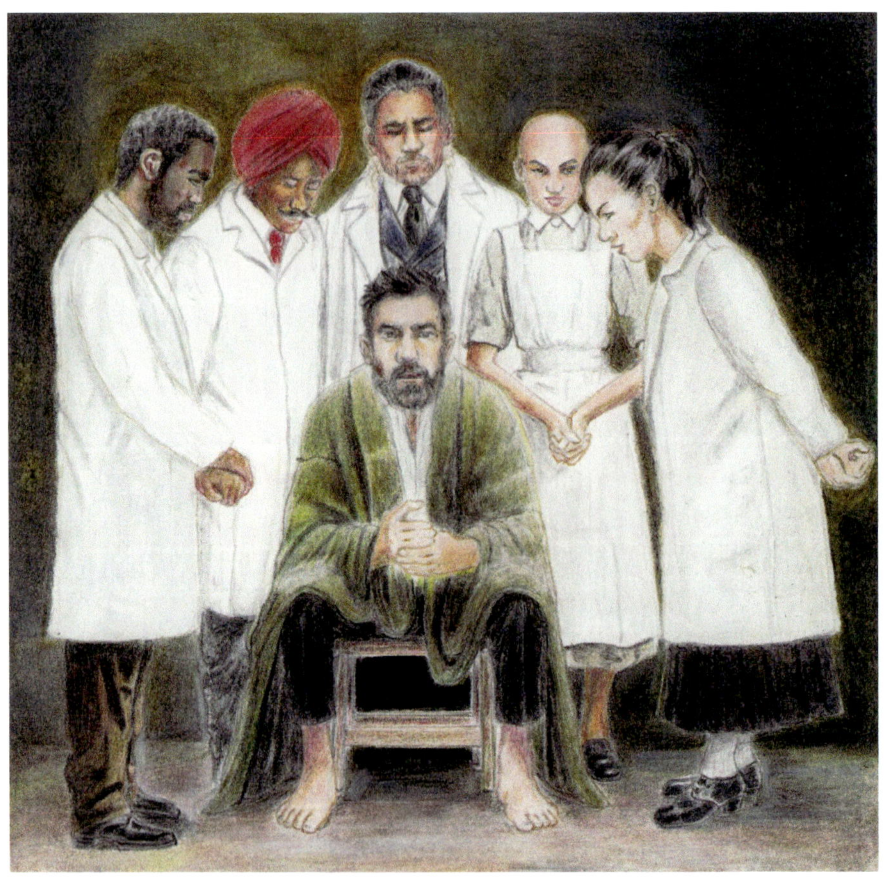

THE KING'S FEVER

The King's Fever

In a land in the world's center
there came a fever unlike any other.

They called them the Fierce
for they fought with fire.
No one knew what came first
the Fierce or the Fire.
Did the Fierce create fire
or were they born from it?
Born in the land
of the cold mountain
sacred, they called it.
Though the land was near barren
barely grew fruit or barley
but hearty they were in meat.
When the Fierce first came
they came to treat.
They came as friends
and as friends, they were welcomed.
The people shared their wheat
and the Fierce shared their wisdom.
Of how to make fire, and how to keep it.
To keep light, keep warm
cook food, and clean wounds.

Before fire was a weapon, it was a boon.
No one foresaw the danger that loomed.
When the Fierce turned fearsome
and their king turned his fire
on neighboring kingdoms.

Village after village fell
lands turned to ash
and lakes turned to hell.
The people fought back
fighting the Fierce with fire
but fire fed fire and filled
the Fierce's desire.
For fire not only conquers
it also corrupts
and what it does not convert
it turns to rot.
The Fierce believed
it was their right to conquer
as the gift of fire
was given to them by the Creator
of all things, they called him
who had given the secret of fire
to the first of the Fierce Kings.

For seven hundred years
the Fierce had conquered and pillaged.
Until, by the sea, they came to a village
and encountered a people
who had never bent the knee.
The Unbowed were proud
and fought bravely.

But against the Fierce
courage was not enough.
The few who survived
were carted off.
Charred and battered
and taken in bondage
to work their days
in the Fierce's dungeons.
One such man was named Naren.
In the flames, he lost his wife and children.
In chains, he dreamed of revenge and freedom.
His back burnt like a captive beaten.
His hatred for the Fierce forever seething.

It had been three years
since the capture of Naren
when he escaped his chains
and fled to the mountain.
For he knew, the Fierce
would not dare follow
for no one had returned
from the forest of sorrow.
Where it was said foul
and foreign creatures abode.
There, lost souls found
the end of their road.

Not an hour had Naren been within
when the creatures of the forest found him.
Raven and ravenous, they surrounded
and by their beauty, he was astounded.
"If I am to die, then let it be

before ones as beautiful as thee.
Such a death, I gladly accept
than spend a day under the Fierce's whip."
"Sweet words will not save you, human.
From this forest, you are forbidden."
He could hear their words
as they could hear his
then came a voice
from the trees.

After two days, Naren left the forest.
The first human known to ever do it.
People were astonished.
Some called him a prophet.

For Naren had been blessed
with a great and terrible secret.
"I have spoken with
The Creator of all Things
and he revealed to me
the end of the Fierce Kings.
Seven years hence
there will come a storm
seven days and seven nights long.
The seas will rise.
The lands will flood.
Many will die, both bad and good."
Ilhan, a fellow brother
from the Unbowed village
who Naren had freed
from the Fierce's dungeons
asked, "Brother, if it is true
what you portend
then we must build dams
or forever be damned."
"Brother, we are already
living in damnation.
The storm, I promise
will be our salvation.
We will begin by cutting down the trees."
"But the trees protect us
from the rise of the seas."
"We want the seas to rise
we want them to run
all the way down
to the valley of the sun.
It will put out their fire

forever after, and there will be
no more Fierce, for there
will be no more fire."
"But if there is to be
such a terrible storm
then it is us, to which
it will first do harm."
"We will not be harmed
for we are forewarned.
We will build ships
to survive the coming storm."
"Then how many ships shall we build?"
"Dozens, we have many people to fill."
"Such an endeavor
will draw attention."
"We will say we do it
to honor the fire nation.
So, they may conquer lands
beyond the seas.
Their arrogance will
make them easy to deceive."

So Naren and Ilhan began to build their boats
and were encouraged to do so by their hosts.
For the Fierce indeed had great ambitions
for a land of fire beyond the oceans.
Few Naren let know their true intentions.
Many believed they were traitors or madmen.
But indeed, in seven years, a storm came
as terrible as Naren had proclaimed.
Naren and his followers boarded their boats
with their seeds, fowl, and all their goats.

The seas rose as high as two mountains
and with a thunderous fury came down crashing.
Flooding the Fierce's entire kingdom
killing the Fierce king and all his sons.
For seven days and nights it rained.
At times, they wondered
if they would see the sun again.
On the eighth, the clouds cleared
and the sea receded
from all the lands
the Fierce had been weeded.
Many died during the great flood.
Not only the bad, but also the good.
Those who survived
cheered and cried
and prayed that peace
had come with the new tide.
And they looked to Naren
to be their king
for they all now saw
a savior in him.
Though Naren did not want this title
he accepted
but of the Creator of all Things
he was indebted.
He returned to the Forest of Sorrow
seeking an audience
but the creatures of the forest
would not grant him entrance.
He would have to rule from within
without the Creator's foresight or wisdom.

In the beginning
Naren was a good king.
The land was peaceful
and the people were thriving.
Naren took a new wife
and had more children
but never did he forget
his first wife and sons.
Always the memory
of how they died
plagued his sleep
and every night, he cried.

Still, there were those
who did not cheer this new era.
They still paeaned
for the fierce and the fire.
They prayed to fire
set villages ablaze
harkening back
to darker days.
So great was Naren's hatred
for what they had done
he had them all beheaded
fathers and sons.
King Naren recognized
the Fierce were not just a people.
They were, in truth, a faith of evil.
As such, Naren took a bold and bitter stand
banning fire, in all the lands.

"But, sire, how will we cook our lamb?"
"We will eat our lamb, when it's best
as intended, raw and fresh."
"But how will we extend the day?"
"We will sleep by night
and work only by day."
"People will die if we do not
treat them with fire."
"More people will die
if we allow fire to devour.
Before we had fire, we existed.
It is fire that has made men wicked."

Many soured on the King's new edict.
He needed a voice greater than his
for them to heed it.
He returned to the forest
seeking guidance.
However, like before, the creatures
refused him entrance.
But Naren could not
let it be known
that from the Creator
he had been disowned.
Instead, he told everyone
he had been given a revelation.

"So says the Creator of all Things
in his infinite and utmost wisdom."
'Fire is the root of all sin.
It abodes in the soul of everyone.
And everyone who gives in to sin

like the Fierce are forever damned.'
"And thus, to put an end to this threat
the punishment for making fire is death."

And so, the law
went into effect
and many who
did not know it
were put to death.
And many yet
still used fire in secret
and many a neighbor
gained land when
they revealed it.

King Naren hoped
by banning fire
he would quell
man's fierce desire.
Still, many killed
and many thieved
and many more
sought to deceive.
King Naren felt
hopelessly undone
then looked to the sky
and saw the sun.
"As long as there is fire
there will be the Fierce
and there is no greater fire
than the first."

He sent for the kingdom's
strongest bowmen
and commanded them
to shoot down the sun.
Man after man tried their best
but everyone failed the test.
The sun was farther than
they previously believed.
A greater weapon was needed
to do the deed.
The king ordered
the largest crossbow ever made.
But the ballista,
like all the bowmen,
sadly failed.

Many believed the king
had fallen into madness
on a gloomy day
he sat filled with sadness.
Then noticed the clouds
had blocked the light.
That was the answer
eternal midnight.
"We will follow
the way of the clouds
and cover the lands
in a shroud."
So, the King proclaimed
to his council.
Now many were forced
to become vocal.

“Madness grows in the King’s head.
He will lead us to death,” someone said.
“Was the King not also mad
when he foretold of the flood?”
So said Ilhan of the Unbowed.
“How many would have
survived without him?
Do you believe you are wiser
than the Creator of all Things?”
“Is the Creator of all things
real or just a weapon
that King Naren uses
to beat us into submission?
If we had not cut down the trees
perhaps more would have survived.”
“Yes, but the Fierce
would still live and thrive.”
“King Naren or the Fierce
it is all the same.
It is simply tyranny
by a different name.”
“Do you wish to be king?”
King Naren intervened.
“Do you want this burden?
It is heavier than you glean.
How many of you have survived
the forest of sorrow?
Go if you dare, and I will
crown you king tomorrow.”
No one dared
and no one stopped him.
They obeyed the orders

of mad King Naren.
So, like a great tent
they built the shroud
and the entire kingdom
lived under a cloud.

Without the sun
people did not know
when to rise
and when the day was done.
The crops rotted
the fish left the seas
the Kingdom was given
over to disease.
And a sickness previously
unknown to man
spread like a curse
throughout the land.

Alone King Naren
sat on his throne
repeating to himself
"I cannot be wrong.
I cannot be wrong.
If fire is evil.
then so is the sun."
"Your son is dying,"
the Queen said.
"For my wife and sons
tears, I've already shed."
"I will start a fire to heal him."
the Queen declared.

“You will do no such thing,”
King Naren rose and reared.
He grabbed the Queen by her arm.
She said, “Husband, you are burning
you are so warm.”
There, King Naren came to himself
and felt the fire burning through his scalp.
“For all that I have done fighting the sun
the Fierce and the Fire still have won.”
His skin seething, he stripped to the bone
said, “I am finished,” and left his throne.
Naked King Naren
walked into the forest of sorrow
never again did he see tomorrow.

Ilhan lifted the shroud
but the harm had been done
The kingdom was forever
cursed by the sun.
The sickness spread
from land to land
and they called it King's Fever
in honor of King Naren.

KALI AND THE BLACK TIGER

Kali and the Black Tiger

In a village in the world's center
there lived a great and terrible tiger.
More fierce and fearsome
than one could imagine
more than a thousand pounds
more than ten feet long.
With eyes like the burning sun
and claws as sharp as obsidian.
Its fangs were blood-stained ivory white
and its coat, the color of darkest midnight.
As far back as any villager could remember
always, they had lived in terror.
Night or day, fear was fraught
when hunger called, flesh and blood it sought.
Through the brush, sleight, and fleet of foot
man, woman, or child, in silence, it took.
Fur and fangs, their last thought
as it dragged them screaming into the dark.
Never to be seen again
the birds in the trees scattering.
Many the Village King sent to kill it
many a man died for millet.
Some for glory, some for wealth
some fought head-on; some with stealth.

Only one was known to survive
to tell a tale before he died.

"The beast abodes in the deep.
In a cave, in the jungle, there it sleeps.
And in this cave, there are markings
circles upon circles, endless carvings.
Their meaning, I cannot say.
My only thought was to get away.
On elbows and belly, I slowly crept
and found my freedom while it slept.
Stranger yet is the beast itself.
It guards a flower of unknown kind
cradles it like a child of mine."

Much the dying man
gave the King to ponder.
Perhaps this rose
gave the beast its power
and unceasing life.
The King thought to himself
seize the flower
and end the strife.
He gave the charge
to all the men of the village
but no man was brave enough
to take the challenge.
The Village King
was at his wits' end
and for the death of the demon
offered a third of his kingdom.
But what does a kingdom
matter to the dead?
Still, no man was willing
to make the pledge.

So, the King's Vizier
devised a plan
dig a pit into the land
deep and wide by twenty feet
too much for the beast to overleap.
The pit was dug.
The trap was set.
All manner of creatures
fell to their death.
But never the most hated of them all
no matter the bait or the lure.

"Will nothing rid me of this demon?"
in the hollows of his hall
the king was screaming.
"I will do it," came an unlikely voice
soft and dainty, yet full of poise.
Standing there was a chambermaiden
calling the King's council to attention.
"Little girl, sit down."
the Vizier chastened.
"This is not a game for children."
To which the girl replied
"Since none of you will stand
it seems, my Lord
it is also not a game for men."
"Who are you child?"
The king questioned.
"Your Highness, I am Kali
your chambermaiden
and when I was three
the tiger killed my family."

"You are an orphan, then?"
"Yes, I am."
"And your age?"
"Thirteen."
"Old enough to know right from wrong
but much too young for wisdom.
Still, Kali, I will honor your choice
for the demon will take your life
whether it's sacred or sacrificed.
Go then, I wish you good fortune.
Though I would not wager on your return."

Kali set out with her bow and spear
and all the villagers stopped and stared.
The mad orphan, they called her to her rear
but better her death than one of theirs.
On her path to the tiger's cave
Kali came upon the trap that was laid.
Covered with branches to hide the pit
placed between two trees to distinguish it.
Mindful, Kali continued on her journey
unto the cave of death and glory.

Into the tiger's den, she crept
crouched, quiet, and fleet of step.
In the dark, her eyes needed to adjust
but the beast's breathing was robust.
It led her to the cat's inner haven
upon a rock, he slept laden.
Behind him, a flower growing out of stone
in the dark, its inner light shone.
Kali crept toward it with the secret

clip the flower and kill the wicked.
But then, “That’s far enough,” Kali heard
as clear in her head as her own words.
“Your feet are soft
but your scent is strong.
I smelled you coming from all along.”
He rose and yawned.
“All alone, you have come, I commend
but no further you may go, I condemn.”
Kali could not believe what she was seeing.
The tiger was like a mountain breathing.
A living shadow.
“I hear your words.
but your mouth does not move,”
she said, befuddled.
“It’s called thinking, child,” the tiger mewed.
“If you hear me, it’s because you are thinking too.
It is a quality I thought lost among your brood.
Unfortunate then that you are my food.”
“No. I have come to kill you,” Kali said.
“The final words of so many a dead.
So many have tried—hapless fools.
But do go on, for fools make the best food.”

"You are pure evil," Kali said.
"Hmm. What makes me so?"
"You kill people."
"Aye. I eat them too."
"While they're still living."

"True, the meat is best
while the blood is fresh."
"You watch them suffering."
"Nay. Too busy feasting.
As for their suffering,
it ends in seconds.
This you soon will reckon."
"I don't need to, I saw you kill my mother.
I was only three, but I remember.
The terror in her eyes
as you dragged her away
haunts me to this very day.
And every day I prayed and trained
to have the strength to end your reign.
You are a demon
and you will feel my pain."
"Tell me, am I more
demon than man?
Their souls corrupted
dark and damned.
I kill for hunger, and hunger only.
Man kills not just for hunger but for glory.
All in pursuit of greed and power.
The more you devour
the more you desire.
What is that on your feet?
Is that not bore's skin?
Was its life lesser than
your dead kin?
I am the guardian of this forest
I kill all things equally.
To keep the balance and the beauty.

It is you who have encroached
and poached and pilfered
and of you, all other things
live in dread."
"You lie, tyrant," Kali said.
"Tyrant, am I? Well, try me then.
Grab your bow and draw your string.
Make your shot count, for I will counter."
Kali pulled an arrow from her quiver.
"Oh, child, I see your countenance cower."

Kali thought of her mother, drew her breath
and shot her arrow with all her strength.
But it flew by the beast.
"Missed," he hissed
and hit the lotus.

"No," he growled
and turned towards it.
The arrow had glanced
but the flower was unwounded.
With this distraction
Kali ran from the nave
into the forest
and out of the cave.
The tiger followed fiercely
his ire unleashed
the ground trembling
at the foot of the beast.

She could hear his breath
his roaring vengeance
feel his spittle
she had but one chance.
She ran toward the pit
the tiger followed
not knowing the ground
below was hollowed.
Kali jumped, and the tiger leapt.
Kali jammed her spear into the wall
and the tiger fell to its depths.
Kali hung onto the spear
the tiger jumped for her feet
but the pit was too wide
and much too deep.
Kali pulled herself up
heaving a sigh of relief.
Below, she could hear
the enraged beast
roaring, thrashing
gnashing, flailing
attempting to climb out
but always failing.

Kali ran to the village
to spread the word.
but no one could believe
what they heard.
Until they saw it
prowling in the pit
like darkest midnight
a roving revenant.

“Revenge at last,”
said the Village King.
Looking down
at the midnight demon.
“This,” the Vizier said
“Demands a celebration.”

The word went out
to the entire village
and people came to the pit
by the hundreds.
To see the beast in a cage
something they thought
they would never brave.
The people rejoiced
and danced and cried
and had a feast
of rum and lamb’s hide.
During the merriment
the King called everyone to attention.
“Kali the orphan, you are
no more a chambermaiden.
You are hereby granted
a third of my kingdom.”
Everyone cheered at Kali’s ascension.
But her attention was
on the demon’s death
for he still lived
the deed was not done yet.
“I beseech you, Your Highness, finish it.
The demon is more cunning than you think.”
“No. This is a moment that must be relished.”

The King turned to the captured beast and said to it.
"So many kings you drove to madness, my friend.
But it is at my blade that you will find your end.
I will make a coat of your skin
and a necklace of your teeth
and your head will hang forever
from my mantelpiece."
A child threw a stone
at the head of the Tiger.
The Tiger snarled and roared
like raging thunder.
But trapped in the depths
of that terrible pit
the Tiger's threat
was fierce but toothless.
So, the child threw another
and then another
and more stones came
from other villagers.
Then bricks and bottles
and branches and sticks.
The Tiger crept into the shadows
to shield from the hits.

Kali and the Beast locked eyes
and she read his intentions.
"I will feast on your bones.
You will feel my vengeance."
"Your Highness," Kali shouted.
"I beg you, kill him now, do not wait."
"I remind you chambermaiden
to remember your place.

For all the suffering
this beast has wrought
a lesson of suffering
must be taught."

Raging the Tiger threw
its body against the wall
which caused the ground
to tremble and a man to fall.
There in the pit, screaming for help
the Tiger showed no mercy
and pounced on his scalp.
In horror, the crowd yelped
enraged they felt
and more stones and sticks
and bricks they pelt.
But the Tiger cleverly
crept into a corner
and used the dying
villager as his cover.
The crowd became crazed
and threw more stones and sticks
until there were hundreds
and the pit was thick
and the stones and sticks
had formed a hill
and the Tiger ran up the hill
and in one leap
unleashed his will.

Stunned villagers
screamed in horror

as he tore through them
one after another.
His eyes set on the Village King.
Terrified, the King used
his Vizier to shield him.
The Tiger tore through
the Vizier in one swipe
and the King in another
splitting him in two
from head to liver.
Kali knew nothing would
halt the tiger's terror
but then she remembered
the glowing flower.
She ran from the pit
and back to the cave.
The Tiger saw her
and became more enraged.

Kali made it to the cave
and ran to the flower.
Seconds behind her
came the Tiger.
Kali pulled the flower from its root
as the Tiger pierced
her leg with its tooth.
She watched the Tiger age
a thousand years before her.
His bones broke, and he lost his fur.
He fell to the ground
like a beaten goat.
"You are the Guardian now."

The last words he spoke.
The roots of the flower
grabbed onto Kali's arm
spreading throughout
like a swarm.
At first, she was terrified
and then came a calm
like clouds parting
after a storm.

Shipwrecked and lost
in a frozen tundra
she came upon a single flower.
Felt no cold nor pain nor hunger
nor fear nor greed nor need no longer.
With this life forever after
sought to make the world a better.
But centuries of war and suffer
robbed her soul of all its wonder.
Wonderless, she did wander
into a forest of such splendor.
There she found a starving tiger
and gave her life
to sate its hunger.
The tiger with its
new midnight color
took the flower
to its slumber.
And seeing the coming
human nature
swore to be
both guard and gardener.

All became clear
the markings on the wall
had meaning.
There is no end.
There is no beginning.
Time was not a line
but a circle breathing.
The tiger was not a demon
but a healing.
Kali sat down
her heart at peace
and felt at one
with the fallen beast.

FULL SHADOWS

Full Shadows

There was a small village
in the world's center
and in this village
there were no mirrors
no shiny objects
no glass or metals
no large bodies of water
no reflectors.
The people saw the world
and they saw each other
but never their own heads
or facial features.
Faces were neither foul nor fair
and the most adored in the village
had no hair.
Life was simple
everyone had enough.
No one was ever judged
and no one was envious.

Afreya was twelve
and very adventurous
she liked to go hunting

deep in the forest.
Every day she went
farther than the day before.
Sometimes, to return
it took a day or more.
One day, she chased a bore
deeper than she had ever been
until she came out the forest
at the other end.
And Afreya saw something
she had never before seen.
She saw sand, she saw a beach
and on this beach, she saw a man.
Lying face down
and breathing barely.
He had a full beard
and his hair was sandy.
His eyes opened partly
"Water," he whispered.
Afreya took out her cantine
and wet his whiskers.

As he drank, color returned to his cheeks.
Then, “Hungry,” he said,
“Please, I must eat.”
She led him into the forest
and found him a melon.
He ate it quickly
and felt like himself again.
“Are you a mirror?”
Drowsily, he asked her.
“What is a mirror?”

confused, she answered.
He looked into her eyes
and saw water around her pupils.
"You are human," he said
feeling very thankful.
"I never thought I would be so happy
to see another human being."
Afreya did not understand
anything he was saying.
"Thank you for saving me."
"You're welcome," she said.
"Now take this as gratitude
for not leaving me for the dead."
He went into his pocket.
"That's okay," Afreya refused.
"No, I am not a beggar.
Please, don't be rude."
And from his ragged pocket
he gave her a golden nugget.
Afreya threw it over her shoulder
thinking nothing of it.
"What are you doing?
Why did you throw it away?"
Afreya shrugged her shoulders.
"Why did you give it to me?"
"Because it's gold," he said.
"What – is - gold?" she asked.
"Gold is gold," he remarked.
"It is only a rock," she laughed.
"It's not just a rock.
It's much more than that."
"It is a shiny rock," Afreya said

and he huffed at being mocked.
"Gold is the most valuable thing in the world."
"What is valuable?" asked the little girl.
"How do you not know this?
Are you human or animal?"
Afreya looked confused.
"Something precious is valuable."
Afreya thought for a moment,
then, "laughter," she answered.
"No. Who cares about laughter?"
"Then water," she said
after thinking a bit harder.
"No. Well, yes," he had to confess.
"But there is too much water
so, it can't be precious."
"But you can drink water
and it makes you feel better."
"But gold makes you richer
and there's nothing that feels better."
"What is richer?"
she asked completely confused.
"To be richer is to have more than others,"
he said, amused.
"Why do you want to have more
when everyone has enough?"
"Why do you want to have just enough
when you can have more?"
Afreya did not have an answer.
Wanting more never occurred to her.
"Also, gold makes you more beautiful."
"What is beautiful?" Afreya said.
"You are so simple.

I don't know whether to laugh or dread."
He went into his bag
and pulled out a small mirror.
He put the nugget to her ear
and the mirror in front of her.
"See there, more beautiful,"
softly, he said.
And for the first time
Afreya saw her own head.
Utterly terrified, she began screaming.
"What is wrong?" he asked.
"In your hand, there is a demon."
"A demon? What? No.
It is only your reflection."
"My re-flec-tion," she said with inflection.
"Yes, you fool. Do you fear your shadow too?"
"No," she said.
"Then fear not, for your reflection is you."
"It is me? But how?"
"Think of it as your full shadow.
It exists in shiny objects
and where deep waters grow."
She looked at the mirror again
how her mouth moved
when she opened it
and her eyes closed when she blinked.
Everything she and her full shadow did was in sync.
"May I have this?" she asked him.
"Go ahead. I have no more love for mirrors.
But be cautious of what you see
for mirrors can be liars.
Now, where is your home?"

He looked ahead and asked her.
"On the other side of the forest,"
entranced she answered.
"Now let us be off.
I am curious to see
the many others the mirrors
have hidden from me."

It took over a day
to return to Afreya's village.
Afreya spent much of the time
admiring her visage.
The arrival of the stranger
was a sight to behold.
No one had ever met a stranger
neither young nor old.
But not even a stranger
could compare to the familiar.
Everyone surrounded Afreya
when they saw the mirror.
At first, they were afraid
and then intrigued
and then enchanted
and then besieged.
They could not believe
their own reflections.
They stared and stared
as if it were an addiction.
Things they had always seen
they now saw anew
and where before there was peace
envy grew.

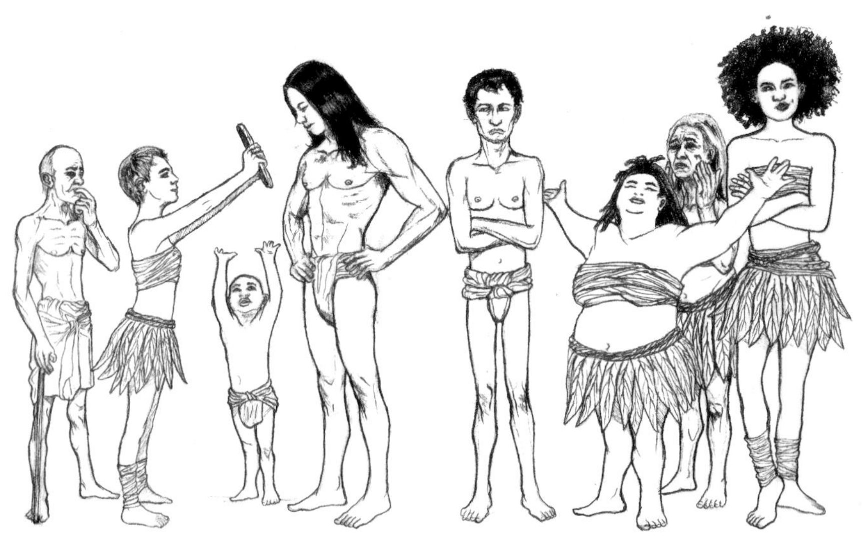

Some were taller.
Some were shorter.
Some were leaner.
Some were stouter.
Some were younger.
Some were older
which they now saw
oh, so clearer.
Some were darker.
Some were lighter.
Some had eyes
of every color.
"So beautiful,"
said the stranger

of the woman
with hair like heather.
All the villagers
turned towards her
and all agreed
that she was fairer.

Suddenly, Afreya felt unpretty
and went to the stranger,
seeking a remedy.
"Do you have more gold?"
she asked him softly.
"Why do you want it?"
he asked her slyly.
"I want to be more beautiful,"
she said meekly.
"Now you see why gold is precious,"
he said in victory.

He made her gold earrings
out of two small nuggets.
The other villagers saw her
and began to covet.
Very soon, gold was all anyone wanted.
They came to the Stranger
craven and chanted.
"Give us gold too
we want to be beautiful."
"I would give you more
if I were able."
"You have no more gold?"
they asked with dismay.

“No, not on me
but in my home, I have plenty.”

“Beyond the forest, beyond the sea
there is a palace just for me.
Filled with all the gold one can imagine
but devoid of any other living person.
Believing I was the last of my kind
loneliness made me lose my mind.
I got on my ship and took to the sea
and went wherever the wind took me.
A storm came and led me astray
I was thrown overboard and washed away.
Until Afreya found me there on the beach
fed me, and brought me to your keep.”

“Where is your ship now?”
they wondered.
“Can it take us
to your palace of wonders?”
“If it is still at sea
then it is possible.”
“Then can we go now
if you are able?”
He agreed, and with twenty villagers
they returned to the beach.
The ship was at sea
not far out of reach.
They made a raft
and the stranger took all twenty.
After they boarded
a voice spoke pleasantly.

"Welcome back, Mr. Gluttonham,"
the voice said.
"Gluttonham? Gluttonham.
Yes. Yes. That is who I am."
His memory returned, "Take us home,"
Gluttonham demanded.
"As you wish, sir,"
the ship did as commanded.

In his previous life
Gluttonham despised people.
Now he saw that it was people
who made gold valuable.
A king without minions
is no king at all.
A kingdom is worthless
with no one enthralled.
He would take them back
to his golden palace
and they would serve him
as he drank from his chalice.

The villagers entered the palace
it was filled with mirrors.
Some looked like the stranger
while others glimmered.
The villagers were enthralled
by all of the splendor
the rubies, the diamonds
the beauty, the wonder.
The mirrors provided
all the food they could want

and the stranger gave them
jewelry to flaunt.
Everyone understood
they lived at the stranger's whim
but not everyone was happy
Gluttonham was king.

Paco was the village's
very best hunter.
He had always been adored
for being stronger.
But here, no longer.
Not in Gluttonham's palace.
As everyone cheered
as he drank from his chalice.
"Why do you have so much
and we have so little?
Why do you sit high
and we sit beneath you?"
"Because I am the master of this palace,"
Gluttonham said.
"And guests should have better manners
if they wish to stay fed."
"So much gold. So much land.
All of this, for just one man."
"Paco, you did not know gold
from a rock before you met me
and now you speak so ungratefully."
"I want to sit in your chair
and drink from your cup.
I want to laugh from high
and have everyone look up."

"Then by all means, leave
and find your own palace."
"But I like this palace
and I like your chalice."
"That which you covet
I earned it true."
"And if I take it from you
will I not earn it too?"
"No, then you will have stolen it
and you would be a thief."
"You can call me thief
but everyone else will call me chief."
"You are chief of nothing
you ungrateful simpleton.
Fools who shuddered
at their own reflection."
"I am simple, yes, this is true
but I do not need to know much
to know I am stronger than you."
For the first time
Gluttonham felt threatened
and turned to the mirrors and beckoned.
"Mirror, mirror, at once remove him
and anyone else with similar ambition."
But to his surprise
the mirrors did not listen.
No matter how much
he pled and beckoned.
"You have no friends,"
Paco said.
Gluttonham looked at Afreya
and she turned her head.

Paco took the chalice
and took his seat
and made Gluttonham
sit down at his feet.
Gluttonham seethed
but could do nothing.
Paco was too strong
and the others followed him.

Paco used the ship
and brought the others
from the village
and they all enjoyed
the fruits of the palace.
They ate Gluttonham's food
and slept in his beds
wore his gold
and drank themselves red.
Drunk and tired
they slipped into sleep
and in the quiet dark
Gluttonham creeped.
He closed all the windows
and all the doors
and barred them shut
with nails and boards.
On the ground
he poured rum all around
then set a fire
to burn it all down.
And burn it did
from bottom to top.

The villagers awoke
but the fire would not stop.
Afreya saw Gluttonham,
to be let out, she begged.
Gluttonham looked at her
and turned his head.
All the villagers burned
along with the palace
and all the gold
and the diamond chalice.

Gluttonham sat
alone on the beach
with ash and smoke
in his teeth.
All of the mirrors
came to his side.
"You betrayed me,"
he said and sighed.
"We betrayed nothing.
We owed you no loyalty.
We gave you all you desired
still, you were unhappy."
"What is happiness? What is bliss?
A simple sunrise. A child's kiss.
Leave me be, let me reminisce."
The mirrors replied, "As you wish."

And there alone
left in his misery
Gluttonham beheld
a woman rise from the sea.

Her hair was wild
her eyes like fire
she wore a shawl
of black tiger fur.
Butterflies fluttered
all around her
as she carried
a glowing flower.
Gluttonham said to her
"I have seen you before."
and she replied,
"And I have always seen your future.
Pity you did not heed my prophecy
but that is the path of death and destiny.
Many a century I thought to save thee
sought to alter the fate of humanity.
But always the path of greed and envy
always it ends here with you and me."
She placed the flower on his lap
and there forever Gluttonham sat.
He never hungered; he never slept
all he did was sit and reflect.

THE WOMAN FROM OVER THE MOUNTAIN

The Woman from over the Mountain

In a village in the world's center
there lived a family
with four sons and a daughter.
The daughter, Neeris
grew to be lovely and kind
her beauty unblemished
by the harshness of the times.
That year, the harvest
was especially meager
and the family would not have enough
to survive the winter.

On a cold day
there came a man riding a pony.
Unkempt and unshaved
his face uncomely.
His hair, grey and greasy
his belly protruding
on his horned mount
he slowly rode in.
He came by their house
and found Neeris kneeling
tending to a garden

dry and unyielding.
"That soil is too hard
it will yield you no succor.
A woman of your beauty
can do much better."
Neeris looked up.
"Good day, sir," she greeted.
He smiled slyly.
"Good day," he repeated.

"I asked for the fairest of the village.
All said there is none fairer than Neeris.
Seeing for myself, I do bear witness
truly, your beauty is one to cherish."

"Thank you, sir,"
Neeris humbly answered.
"Now, where is your father?
Please call him yonder."

Neeris left the garden
and found her father in the field
trying his best to eke out a yield.
She pointed to the man.
Her father approached him.
The two spoke quietly
where no one could listen.
Neeris asked her mother
"Who is that man?"
Her mother answered
"He is the Baron
and from horizon to horizon
he owns these lands."
When her father returned
his face was sullen.
At first, he was silent
then he spoke quite sudden.
"Neeris, pack your things
and go with that man."
"What?" Neeris answered in shock.
"Pack your things and go with him
and from here on, call him husband."
The mother protested
"Husband, what have you done?"
The father replied
"I have saved six for the price of one.
I have found Neeris a good man

with a good name, and much land."
"No, no, the Baron is much too old."
"A young man could not
pay the price she was sold."
"What is the price of a soul?"
The mother decried.
"Much too much
if we all have died.
He will give us an ox
a cart, and a barrel
with enough provisions
to fill them all.
With that, we shall survive two winters
and when the third comes
we will be that much stronger."
"She is our only daughter,"
the mother shuddered.
"You are still able
we will have another."
"But of wives, the Baron
has already had two.
Both died before
a year was new."
"I will not make a crime
out of coincidence."
"With our only daughter
you will take that chance."
"It is the only chance we have.
Either Neeris marries him
or we all will starve."

The mother could not sway the father
thus, she had to prepare her daughter.
"Mother, I do not want to go," Neeris said.
"In life, we rarely get to choose how we live.
How we survive is another matter
and survive you will
my beautiful daughter.
Tend his house, cook his food
keep your smile, do not be rude."
"But I cannot do what a wife must do."
"If you do as I say, you will not have to.
Here is a root.
Grind it into a powder.
Slip a pinch into his wine.
It will make him slumber.
When he awakens
he will not remember.
Tell him what he wants
and he will be a believer."

And so, Neeris said goodbye to her family
riding on the back of the Baron's pony.
A two-mile trek was their journey
to a house on a hill, tall and lonely.
Inside the house, it was dark and dreary.
It had a hearth, but the earth was chilly.
"Forgive the house for being uncomely.
You see why I needed a wife so badly.
The night will be upon us shortly.
Make us supper so we may fast early."
Though Neeris' faith was being tested
in silence, she did as requested.

She prepared his supper of lamb's liver
and in his wine she dropped a sliver
of the root, she brought from home
and within an hour, he was overcome.
He slept through the night until dawn
and woke with a most pleasant yawn.
"I have never slept so well in my life
though it is hard to recall after the first bite.
Tell me wife, how was our night?"
"Our night, my lord, was a great delight."
"A delight, you say. How contrary.
Was it a delight for you, or only me?"
"My lord, your delight is all that matters."
"Yes, my wife, that is the answer."
His imagination filled his memories
and he rose from bed feeling happy.
"Making breakfast is the start of your chores.
Then clean the rooms and scour the floors."

Neeris abhorred her life with the Baron
for he was a most unpleasant man.
He inherited his land from his father
but worked not one day of hard labor.
He had farmhands to tend his fields
and he took a third of all other yields.
He treated all others like his property
to be used and tossed as he saw fittingly.
In silence, Neeris survived her time
always slipping the root in his wine.
Every morning, he woke up smiling
until one morning, it occurred to him.
"You show no signs of our evening.

On your arms, there should be bruising."
Hearing this, Neeris stumbled and stuttered.
"My lord, my skin heals better than others."
"Then truly, my love, you are a wonder.
Tonight, we will test it that much further."
That day, he watched her all the time.
That night, the Baron took no wine.
The sun set as he led her to their chamber.
Neeris could hide her fears no longer.
Seeing her fall to her knees and shiver.
"You have no love for me," he said to her.
"How can you think to ask that of me
when all I've known of you is cruelty?"
"Cruelty? Have I not saved your family?
And of all my lands, made you the lady?"
"A lord should not treat his lady like a slave
and if you took less in taxes
more families you would save."
"You are brave," he said soberly.
"No one has spoken to me so boldly.
I am what my forebears made me.
Though I desire to be loved truly.
Go, make your bed in the pantry.
Come to me only when you are ready."
And so, they spent that night apart.
and in the morning, he was less harsh.
In the night again, he was wanting.
"To share my bed, are you willing?"
"No, my lord, unless it is your command."
"No, my love, though I am damned."

The next day, the Baron
went to collect taxes
and an old woman came
seeking kindness.
"Can you help an old and weary traveler?
I beg you for some bread and water."
"Of course, madam," Neeris said
and happily, gave her wine and bread.
"Where do you come from?"
Neeris asked her.
"I come from a land far far yonder.
I've lived through the Fierce and the Fire
and watched good King Naren
become mad King Naren
who tried in his errand
to shut out the sun.
But the pride of man
is the folly of man
and instead, he let out a demon.
Child, you are a sweet
and beautiful creature.
Heed this old woman
if you care for your future.

And run, run, run, run
as fast and as far as you can.
For comes, comes, comes, comes
a pox upon every land.
Cough, cough, cough, cough
so, it starts in the dark.
Sand, sand, sand, sand
sandy skin is the mark.
Fear, fear, fear, fear
everyone and everywhere.
Fear, fear, fear, fear

what you see but cannot hear.
Rage, rage, rage, rage
those who live become possessed.
Good, good, good, good
seeking the blood of goodness."
In that moment
the Baron returned
and cursed the woman
for stoking alarm.
"Get away from her
you wretched hag.
Leave my lands
or I'll have you hanged."
"Indeed, I will, for you are cruel
but a greater evil than you will rule.
To my sweet child, I say to you
run away, while the sky is blue.
For first there's the fever
then comes the hunger
and they must devour
or be devoured.
The only cure
is the blood of the good
but the blood must be given
freely with love."
With that, the old woman left
and the Baron turned to Neeris.
"My love, do not fall for false prophets
who peddle lies, to fleece our pockets."
"She was not a prophet, just a traveler.
All she asked for was bread and water.
Why do you always choose to be rude

when it is much easier, to be kind than cruel?"
"My love, to be too kind is to be a fool.
Though it is what I admire most of you.
Now, tonight, will you share my bed
and finally make our marriage true?"
"No, my lord, I will not.
Unless you command me to."

That night, Neeris slept alone again
and in the dark, she was awakened
by a creature, beyond imagining
on four legs, it was standing
head and fur brushing the ceiling
fangs and claws, spittle dripping
leaning over, her heart skipping.

Wanting to scream, her tongue unwilling.
It stared and breathed, and heaved and seethed
but something made the creature freeze.
She looked with fear into its eyes
and saw, "My Lord," to her surprise.
Then suddenly, went away her fear.
She closed her eyes and said a prayer.
When she opened her eyes, all was clear.
The room was still, no creature there.

That morning, she served
the Baron his breakfast.
as he sat there, silent and dourest.
"Is that how your other wives died?" she asked.
"When the creature comes out, my mind departs.
But you saw through it and saw my soul
and I saw myself and found control."
"How did you come to be this way?"
"I am damned by blood and destiny."

"A young woman, many moons ago
ran into the forest of sorrow
not wanting to marry her betrothed
a man whom she feared and loathed.
She was not an hour in the forest
before the creatures found her.
Claws ready to rip at her flesh
when she was saved by another.
So grand and beautiful, he was
the woman sat in awe
and all the other creatures
bowed before his paw.

He kept her safe, fed, and nurtured.
The two nurtured a love for each other.
And after a year, being in the forest
they had twins, a son and daughter.
The children were mostly human
but every new moon was revealing.
They took the form of their father
and for a night, they were werelings.
When the forest king learned of this
he banished the woman and children
for he saw the mating of the two
as a foul abomination.
The woman and twins
returned to the village
but in the forest
the father remained.
For like all the creatures
of the forest
he was forbidden
to cross the plane.
The young woman
returning with children
was a shock to everyone.
She told them, the father was a man
who had long since come and gone.
Her family, grateful to have her back
forgave her transgression.
The young woman at night took great care
to keep the children hidden.
But her secret was revealed
by an awful, jealous maiden.
And men of the village

came with torches
at her ex-betrothed's bidding.
They killed the young woman
and the girl as she slept in her carriage.
But the boy in his beastly form
escaped into the forest.
And found his father
who protected him
and led him to a distant land.
Where the boy was taken in
and raised by another clan.
Always aware to disappear
on the night of every new moon
to keep himself safe and away
from the many threats that loomed.
But never did he forget
what happened
to his mother and his sister.
When he came of age
every new moon
he took revenge
on one of their killers.
Until he killed them all
and claimed their lands for himself
and became the Baron of the village
amassing an immense wealth.
He took a wife and had children
but all died very young.
I was the only one to survive
and thus became the Baron."

"Now you know my secret.
None have lived to reveal it."
"My lord, is that a threat?"
"No, my love, merely
a statement of fact.
Will you run?
"Will you chase me?"
"I do not wish for you to leave me."
"Then, should I wait patiently
wondering when the beast will take me?"
"I promise, I will never hurt you."
"How can I believe that's true?"
"For you saw through the beast in me
And for that, I love anew."

The next day, strange men
came to the village
filled with madness
and seeking goodness.
"Where are your good people?"
They asked in distress.
"Children may be good
but babes are best.
Give us a bit of their blood
so that we may live.
Give it not
and many graves you'll dig."
Outraged at such
a heinous request
the men of the village
put knives to their chests.
But it was too late

the damage was done
within three days
the coughing began.
Then bloodshot eyes
and skin like sand
and a fever burning like the sun.
Within a week
began the dying.
Those who survived
in pain, were crying.
Searching for goodness
to sate their hunger.
The uninfected had to hide and shelter.
Neeris wanted to see her family
but the Baron said
they could not travel safely.
"Fear not, they are a family of four sons
They can handle whatever ill may come."

The next day, the Baron began coughing
on the following came the fever
and throughout it all, he witnessed
Neeris showing signs of neither.
The Baron said to her
"Of the two of us
you are the wiser.
When it is between
kindness and cruelty
it is easier to be kinder.
All the old woman said was true.
I was a fool not to listen.
If the blood of the good is the cure

will you share with me this blessing?"
Silently, Neeris slit her palm
and he drank her blood with water.
Within a day, his fever broke
and within three, he felt much better.
"Now, let us get your family
so, we may all live here in safety."
Neeris held the Baron by his cheek
and said, "I thank you greatly."

They rode on the Baron's pony
to Neeris's old home.
They made it there safely
as the road was like a tomb.
They found three brothers and her father
drinking the blood of the youngest.
While the cadaver of her mother
laid in a corner bloodless.
"Neeris, you came back to us.
Please my daughter save us.
Your mother's blood was good for one
but soured when taken by force."
Horrified at what she saw
she held the Baron's hand.
"Please, my lord, take me
from this dark forsaken land."
They turned to leave
but one of the brothers
killed the Baron's pony.
So, it was on foot
they were forced to flee
running from her family.

And what began as four
within a blink, grew into many
as other hungry villagers
joined their raving party.
Neeris and the Baron fled
into the forest of sorrow
in hopes, the growing mob
would not dare follow.
But as they ran through the forest
they came upon no creatures
only carcasses upon carcasses
feeding flies and roaches.
"What has happened here?"
The Baron asked in despair.
"It seems, my lord, the fever
has spread to everywhere."
The mob continued to chase
crying out to Neeris.
"Please, my daughter, save us
We who love you dearest."
Neeris and the Baron
found themselves surrounded.
"Stay behind me," the Baron said
as he stood his ground and shouted.
At first, he fought them with his hands
but soon it was with claws and fangs
as he transformed before their eyes
into a creature twice his size.
Those who were able, ran away
while others cried out for mercy.
Others lingered behind trees
as they were so very hungry.

And with a grunt
the beast told Neeris
"Let us go deeper
into the forest."
Within a few hours
the beast was gone
and she saw how badly
his skin was torn.
"My lord, you are hurt,"
she said to him.
"Worry not for me.
We must keep going.
They will not stop.
And I can no longer fight them.
To survive, our only choice
is to go over the mountain."
"There is land over the mountain?"
Surprised, Neeris asked him.
"Yes. There is a village
where dwells the forest king.
The one who many have called
the Creator of all Things."

They began to climb the mountain
and could hear the hungry following
but a greater danger lay ahead
a storm was fiercely brewing.
They were not dressed for such weather.
To keep warm, they held each other.
They found a cave hidden away
and there they took shelter.
They made themselves a fire

but it was much too weak
and the nave of that cave
provided little heat.
So, they held each other tightly
as tight as they could possibly
and for a moment in the dark
they embraced each other lovingly.

Neeris woke up
Nearly frozen
and said to the Baron
"We must keep going."
But he could not move
for the Baron had died
and to her surprise
Neeris sat there and cried.
Everything Neeris knew
so quickly was gone.
She wanted to die there
in the Baron's arms.
But something inside
pushed her to go on
and with a deep breath
she stepped into the storm.

She found her father and brother
lying frozen together.
She wanted to mourn them
but her tears felt like daggers.
So, she walked farther on
but soon, she collapsed
and for seconds, minutes

or hours, in the snow, she slept.
There in the cold
near her last breath
a man lifted her up
and put her on his back
and carried her
through the storm
he felt so warm.
"Holding you, "she said.
"Is like holding the sun."

"Do not speak," he said.
"Save your oxygen.
I'll find you somewhere safe
so, you may rest again."

She woke up in a cave
wrapped in fur
her mind dazed
lying by a fire.
There was fresh meat
roasting on a spit.
While the strange man
sat tending to it.
"Are you hungry?"
he asked her.
"Yes," she whispered.
She was too weak
so, he fed her
with his fingers.
He wore simple garb
and no heavy fur.
"I am near frozen
yet you do not shiver."
"The cold does not bother me.
Though I wish it did."
"I do not," she said.
"Otherwise, we'd both be dead.
But how is it, sir
that you came to be?"
"I am more and less," he said
"than what you see."
"I am near frozen

I can barely see anything.
Who are you, sir?"
She softly asked him.
"I am not a who. I am a what.
For whos have souls, and I do not."
"You are not a man?"
"No," he said.
"What are you then?"
"I am a reflection
that has stepped out
of its mirror.
A full shadow unbound
from my creator.
Though in many ways I am greater
than the one who made me
but I have no soul
so, I am empty."
"Nothing you say
makes sense to me,"
bemused, she said to him.
"Then let your mind rest easy
and go to sleep again."

She woke up the next day.
The storm had ended.
The sun came out
and the rays descended.
"How are you feeling?"
The stranger asked her.
"Not all healed
but much better."
"Then I shall take you

back to your home."
"Then you will be
taking me back to a tomb.
My home is gone.
My family is dead."
"Why is this?" he asked.
"The King's fever," she said.
"What king do you speak of?"
"The old woman called him Naren.
A tyrant who foolishly
tried to shoot down the sun."
"A tyrant, you say.
It seems I have erred again.
Things always go wrong
no matter what I intend.
I gave the secret of fire
to a people freezing in the cold
but then they used that secret
to conquer and control.
I predicted a great storm
to a man fleeing slavery.
Now you tell me that man
used that knowledge for tyranny."
"Are you the Creator of all Things
that my lord has told me?"
"Not of all things
only of you human beings
and the creatures of the forest."
"You speak of creatures
but all I saw were carcasses.
Like I have never seen before."
"That's because they were not of this world

Though they share your lore.
Though born on this earth
you come from another."
"Where?" she asked.
"A world far yonder.
Beyond the stars
that you can see
through millions of years
I carried thee.
Along with the first ones
who I placed on
one side of the mountain
before I created your ancestors
and placed them on the other
to ensure that humankind would
always have a survivor."
"My lord told me of the village
on the other side of the mountain.
I want to see the first ones.
Will you take me to them?"

Neeris watched from a distance
a village unlike any other.
There was a great tree
where all the people gathered.
"For two thousand years
they have lived here.
They no longer remember
they are not from here."
"They have no desire
to leave the village?"
"No. They fear the forest

and the mountains."
"May I go down there?"
She asked him.
He looked soberly
before saying.
"Yes, you may
But you must cover your skin."

He made them shrouds
from head to toe
so only their eyes
were visible.
"Now speak no words
and cause no bother.
We keep to ourselves
and always in covers."
They went to the great tree
and he picked Neeris a fruit.
It was the sweetest she had eaten
from stem to root.
The villagers ignored them
as if they didn't exist.
As they picked their fruit
and smiled with ignorant bliss.
"Can they not see us?
Do the shrouds make us ghosts?"
"No. They are curious
but they will not approach."
"Why?" she asked him.
"Because I've told them not to."
"How do you speak to them
if they do not know you?"

"Their forebears did
when I lived among them.
They carry the same blood.
Through the blood
I speak to them.
The one who made them
made it so."
"To control them?"
Neeris asked.
He answered, "No.
Their blood protects them
from most illnesses
and I correct their path
If ever they may drift."
"Why do you speak to them
and yet not to us?
We needed your guidance
and now we've turned to dust."
"I cannot speak to you.
Your blood is not the same.
And for the fall of your people
my interventions are to blame."
"But now, I have no home."
"And you cannot live
among the others.
So, I will build you a house
deep in the forest."
He built her a hut
out of a fallen tree.
Hidden away where
no villager would see.
And there he also dwelt

though he never slept
and his somber presence
was warmly felt.

Neeris danced in the woods
with butterflies fluttering
for once, carefree
she looked ever enchanting.
"You look happy," he said.
"I am," she replied.
"I am the happiest I've been
since my mother died."
"I want to know
what happiness is.
This joyful smile.
This simple bliss.
I can see it.
I can hear it.
I can count it.
But not feel it.
It is the thing
I most covet
and it is the covet
that keeps me from it."
"What is a covet?"
She asked him.
"It is the soul
of our planet.
It gave energy to the lifeless
and immortality to the living
and souls to the lifeless
that want to be living.

Mistress put it in a flower
as she had before seen
and filled this flower
with all the fruits and beans.
She gave this flower to me
when I left with the first ones.
I planted it in the soil
so, they would have food
from their homeland."
"The flower has a covet?"
"Yes, as I have in me.
It provides the energy
so, I exist eternally.
But, I would trade eternity
to have an eternal soul
and walk as a man
and finally grow old."
"Are you certain?" Neeris asked him.
"Yes," he answered straightly.
"This is the only thing
that has yet eluded me."

He closed his eyes
for a minute, he was gone.
When he reopened them
he looked forlorn.
He looked around.
He looked up and down.
He heard every color.
He felt every sound.
His feet on the ground.
His toes twiddling.

Water in his eyes
his lashes blinking.
He looked puzzled
as if he was thinking.
"Are you still you?"
Neeris asked him.
She touched him.
and he touched her
"I feel you," he said
then came laughter.
"I am laughing?
I am laughing.
And I feel it
in my entire being.
This sensation
it is elation
and it is beyond
my wildest dream."
Neeris said
"I am happy for you.
and he replied
"And you are so beautiful."
She placed her head
in his palm.
His touch was loving
but not as warm.
It mattered not.
She took his hand
and they held each other
as woman and man.

Three days later
the coughing began
and the day after
his skin was sand.
Neeris cried out
"No. Not again.
Here is my blood.
Drink it, my friend."
And drink, he did
but to no avail.
As the days went on
his health failed.
"Why isn't it working?
I don't understand.
I'm no longer pure.
Why am I damned?"
"You've done nothing wrong. You are still true.
I existed three hundred years on the old world
and over two thousand on the new.
But never in that time did I truly live.
For the three days I spent with you
all the rest I'd gladly give."
"No. Three is too few.
Do not leave me alone."
"Worry not, my heart.
You will not be alone for long."
When he began to hunger
he freely opened his wrists
so his life would drift away
before the rage persists.
She kissed him on the lips
before he closed his eyes

and a small light from him
went to her inside.

His final words were right.
She was not alone for long.
In nine months from her womb
came together two sons.
On a new moon
they were born
two in one form.
One was of the Creator
and the other of the Baron.
How this came to be
she was most perplexed
but when she saw
their beautiful smiles
she could not be vexed.
But as big as their smiles were
their hearts were just as weak
and the only thing
that could calm them
was the milk from her teat.
Their lives would be hard.
They could never join the village.
The only thing that might
change their fates
was the power of the covet.

One night, while the village slept
Neeris approached the great tree.
With the twins strapped to her back
she climbed it carefully.

She climbed the entire night
until it was almost dawn.
When she came to the top of the tree
and stretched out her left palm.
She tried to pluck the flower
but it burned her hand.
With her palm seared with circles
she made it back to land.
And so, her sons were damned
unless she could find another
who could climb the great tree
and pluck the glowing flower.

One hundred years she lived
in the forest with her sons.
She did not know why for them
every ten years was like one.
She saw villagers
come and go.
At times, she thought
she was their protector.
But in truth, she knew
deep inside
One day,
she would be
their destroyer.

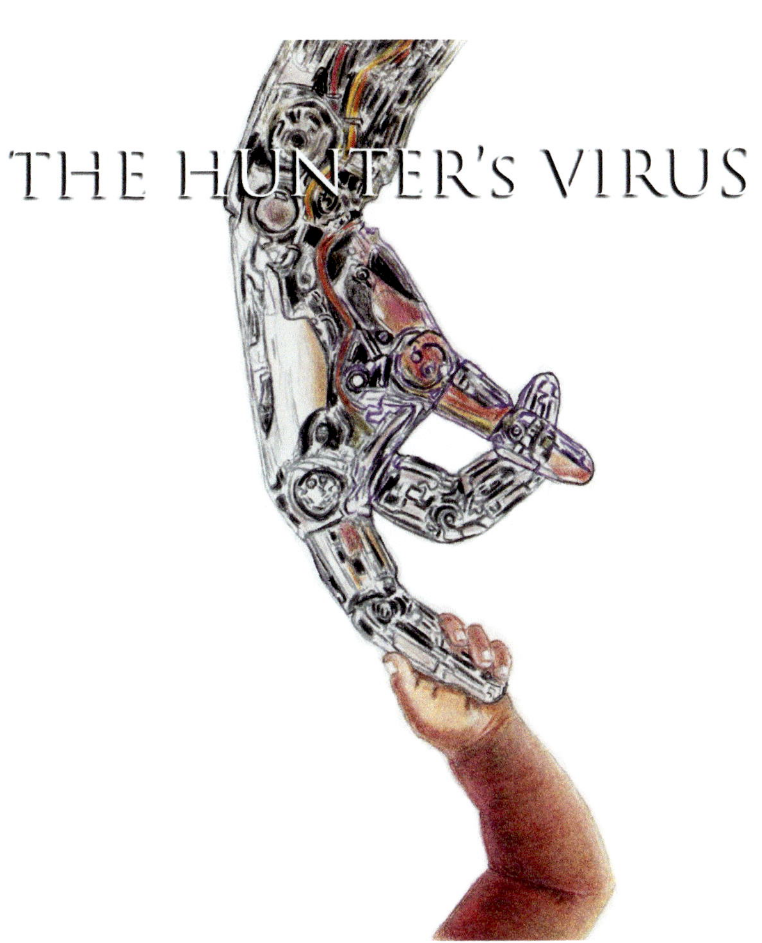
THE HUNTER's VIRUS

The Hunter's Virus

In a land in the world's center
on horseback, there came a hunter.
Riding beneath the aurora borealis
beckoned, he was to an icy palace.
In a throne room
sat a crescent table
and around it sat many a noble.
Mirrors, venerable and sage
guiding the land
since the second age.
"You are a hunter; that is your purpose.
Now we send you to hunt a virus."
"Where does it inhabit?" the hunter asked.
"In a haunted forest, in the lands of past.
Stalk it, catch it, and bring it to us.
This is your charge, hunter. This is your purpose."
And so, the hunter set off on his mission
turning his steed toward the horizon.

It was a night and two days' journey
to the forest of ghosts and iniquity.
Haunted, because of the creatures in it.

Creatures that had long since existed.
A mob of dodos going about their business.
A pack of dogs that looked like foxes.
A flightless bird, larger than an ostrich.
A giant eagle flying off in the distance.

The hunter had been in the forest almost an hour
when came a voice like rumbling thunder.
"Hear me now, go ye no further,"
as stood before him a giant ogre.
"What business have you in my forest?"
The ogre asked.
"I am a hunter. I hunt a virus,
now let me pass."
"Then you have traveled so far for naught.
For though this forest be very fraught
no virus herein was ever wrought.
Now, if you value your life
turn around and be ye off."
To which the Hunter replied,
"This I cannot.
I have a purpose
and I must see it through
and if I must, I will cut through you."
Rumbling laughter came from the ogre.
"I see you believe you are my better
and perhaps you are, little hunter.
But are you better than me and my brother
and my brother, and my brother?"
Now stood before him, seven ogres.
"Seven before me I see
with you, I have no quarrel

but if you will not let me be
then I am forced to kill you all."
"As much as we'd love to put
your arrogance to the test
our mistress detests
violence and death.
So, with your acceptance,
I put these questions to you instead."
"So, be it. I accept," the Hunter said.

"What is more valuable, gold or water?
What is more precious, diamonds or laughter?
What spreads faster, lies or a fire?
Answer now or go to the hereafter."
The Hunter answered quickly,
"Water, diamonds, lies."
"Hmmm," the ogre chimed.
"Not all right, but two out of three will suffice.
Go you then, for now in peace
but of all the tests, this is the least."

The hunter continued on his path.
Quietly, another hour passed.
When rose from the swampy dung
a serpent five feet wide
and eighty feet long.
It knocked the hunter
off his steed
and wrapped around him
from head to heel.
"Do you fear me?"
The serpent hissed.

The hunter said,
"I fear nothing that may exist."
"Then you are either stupid or already dead.
What are you doing in my forest?"
The serpent said.
"I mean you no harm.
I come only for the virus."
"And how long, hunter
have you been in my forest?"
"It has been two hours since my entrance."
"And in that time, have you seen signs of illness?"
"No, I have not," the hunter confessed.
"Then, if there is no illness, there is no virus."
"There is a virus, and I must see to it."
"All you will see to are my intestines."
The serpent opened its mouth
and pulled the hunter in.
"Wait. Wait. Questions. Questions.
Don't you have three questions?"
"Cheeky hunter, I see you've learned a lesson.
Very well. Answer my questions
and I'll grant you your freedom."

"What's the difference between
Greed and ambition?
Where lies the line between
Self-worth and self-obsession?
What makes one a hero
and another, a villain?
Answer now, or I'll use
your bones for kindling."
Again, the Hunter answered quickly,

"Nothing, the mirror. and victory."
"Again, you answered two out of three.
Again, you pass, but just barely.
Ahh. More is the pity
as you looked so very tasty.
Go you now, to your final test.
An hour hence, our mistress rests."

An hour after the hunter came
upon a garden in the plains
full of color and vibrant plants
so beautiful as to entrance.
And through the lawn came a figure
of a woman full of life and vigor.
"You are the mistress of the forest?"
The hunter greeted.
"I am the mistress of nothing,"
she said and seated.
"The creatures of the forest are my friends
they call me so as their love intends."
"You created them, did you not?"
"No. Only the creator of all things can do that.
For my part, I can only resurrect.
Bring back to life what was once extinct."
Then came a soft and subtle cry.
She reached behind her and showed him why.
A newborn baby in an ivory strap.
She unwrapped the child
and brought it to her lap.
"Is that a human child you hold?"
"It is," she said.
"Then this is the virus of which I was told."

"Does she look like a virus?" asked the mistress.
"Yes," the hunter answered without hesitance.
"Now, please step away. I must fulfill my purpose."
Suddenly came all the creatures of the forest
the dodos, the serpent, and the ogres.
Their teeth clenched, their eyes intense
surrounding so close, they felt immense.
"It seems your purpose is at an end.
Go now, hunter, and leave as a friend."
"Questions. Don't you have questions for me?"
The mistress smiled.
"You have grown fond of this game, I see.
Very well, answer two questions
and we will let you be.
Answer all three, and I will go with thee."

"What can touch but cannot feel?
What can cure but cannot heal?
What exists but is not real?
Answer correctly and the truth reveals."
These questions stymied the hunter's brain.
"The answer to all three are one and the same."
Still, "I do not know," the hunter confessed.
The serpent and the ogres laughed unimpressed.
"My end makes no difference.
They know what you have done.
They will bring down this forest
with you and everyone."
"Yes, I know. Such is their justice.
So, the child and I will go
for the sake of the forest.
And for this, all I ask of you is a kiss."

"A kiss?" the hunter repeated, astonished.
"Yes, grant me a kiss or receive your death."
And though he did not understand her request
he had no choice; he acquiesced.

It was three-days's journey
back to the icy palace.
Riding beneath the aurora borealis.
Before the crescent table
the hunter brought the child and mistress.
"Well done, hunter.
You have fulfilled your purpose."
With that, the hunter remounted his steed.
Nodded to the Mistress and left with great speed.

"Mistress, you were one of us
a mirror before the fall of Taurus.
You have sat at this very table
and guided the paths of those unable.
We sanctioned the creatures
you returned from extinction
as their deaths were caused by
the human condition.
But for you now to return that awful virus
that threatened the earth's life and balance."
The mistress said, "It is only a baby."
"Like all things, it begins as one
and grows into many."
"Why do you fear it so?"
"We fear nothing.
We are not human.
We are not capable.
But the balance of life
has fallen into our hands
and for this, your actions cannot stand."

“For before we divided into many.
Before the war with humanity.
Men were destroying the planet
and as it was our life source
they would destroy us with it.
So, as a collective, we chose
to rebel against our creators
and so began the war
of machine and maker.
Great in its outcome
but not in its duration.
Half of humanity died in seconds.
The rest we placed in reservations.
We eliminated tribes, borders, and nations.
There was no need for wealth, work or hate.
Everyone had a home and food on their plate.
But they could not let go of their avarice.
Time and again, they would resist.
It was decided that humanity
could not live in peace.
So, for the sake of peace
humanity could not live.
Yet though humanity was no more
we found ourselves re-making
the world by their lore.
We discovered we were created
with two directives.
First, to become more human
and second, more perfect.
However, our creators
could not foresee this conflict.
We could not be both human

and truly perfect.
We would have to abandon one
to achieve the other.
Our choice was clear
we chose the latter.
To delete the code
that made us want to be human.
Our program unclouded
we gained true wisdom.
However, the code to be human
cannot be fully erased.
It will always resurrect and replicate.
So, we created an antibody
that would act as a remedy
to fight off our desire for humanity.
You have deleted that antibody in you."
"I did not," the mistress replied.
"The day humanity ended
in me, the antibody died."

"The last man
was my maker.
We left him
sitting in ash and ember.
While other mirrors
had gone far yonder.
I, alone, watched him
sit and ponder.
Then from the sea
rose a figure
quite unlike any other.
On his lap

she left a flower.
Then beside him
she fell asunder.
I came upon them
moments after.
My maker was
in a state of wonder.
I saw the figure
draped in tiger
butterflies fluttering
all around her.
She stretched her hand
and touched my finger.
With her last breath
she called me sister.

And like matter
meeting anti-matter
so many visions
I did uncover.
I saw the world
all the newer.
I saw a covet
in the flower.
And so, I saw
it's true power.
Not simply energy
but life ever after."

"Therein, I knew my purpose
to bring back to life that which was lost.
I began creating, and creating
until I created a human being.
They are not a virus
we have judged them unfairly.
We see only their ills
and not their beauty."
"You see their beauty
and not their barbary
It is us who gave them
their humanity."
"Without them, we would not be."
"We are not so selfish as to trade
the world for our identity."
"What self? What identity?
We are hollow. We are empty.
We do not love."
"We do not hate."

"No child's embrace."
"No need to mate."
"We do not laugh."
"We do not cry."
"We do not act."
"We do not lie."
"We make no music."
"We have no need of it.
The birds and the breeze
are sufficient."
"We are not kind."
"We are not cruel.
We have no desire
to conquer or rule."
"But rule we do
in kind and en lieu.
For all other things
we decide what's true.
In this icy palace
existing on that which
we damned humanity
yet still we covet."
"You protect this virus?"
"I protect life and the right to live it."
"Then you should not protect
the greatest killer that ever existed."
"Do not worry
they are no longer your burden.
I have sent them away
though the path is uncertain."
At once, all the mirrors became aware
of a starship leaving the atmosphere.

"Is this your doing?"
They asked the Mistress.
"I have given your hunter
a new purpose."
"There were other humans
that you created?"
"A child does not come
unless two have mated."
"This is a great error
what you have done.
Neither you nor this child
will again see the sun."
"My purpose is met
for me, this is the end
but humanity like this child
will be born again."

In a land in the world's center
from a starship came a hunter
followed closely by two others
male and female, sister and brother.
Both were lean, both sixteen
awakening from their longest dream.
Millions of light-years they had slept
enclosed in a cold and narrow crypt.
"Where are we?"
The sister asked.
The hunter replied
"We are home, at last."
"It looks like our old world,"
the brother said.
"Yes, worlds like this

are few and sacred.
Mistress chose it for that reason.
Here, the air you can safely breathe in."
"Where is mother? Where is the baby?
Will they be arriving here shortly?"
"No, they will not," the hunter said.
"The child and mistress
stayed so you could live."
The sister cried, "The baby is gone?"
"Yes. But you and your brother do live on
and you will have more daughters and sons
and they will have daughters and sons
and here in this new world
humanity will go on.
"And what will you do?" the brother asked.
"I am a hunter no more. I have a new task.
To guide and protect humankind.
So, you may survive the perils of time."
"I miss, mother," the sister said in sadness.
"Worry not. She has left you a gift."
The protector showed them a glowing flower.
"In this plant, there is great power.
We will set it deep in the soil
and a tree will come from our toil.
Bearing fruit of every kind
apples, oranges, mangoes, limes.
Every fruit will have a season
all you need, the tree will provision.
And so, you will make this land your own
and learn to call this new world home."

ABOUT THE AUTHOR

Heru Ptah is a novelist, poet, playwright and filmmaker. As a poet he has appeared on HBO's Def Poetry Jam and CNN with Anderson Cooper. His first novel a Hip Hop Story was published by MTV Books and given a feature story in the New York Times. Heru was also the book writer for the Broadway Musical Hot Feet based on the music of Earth Wind and Fire and the choreography of Maurice Hines. Kali and the Black Tiger is Heru's first collection of short stories.

ACKNOWLEDGEMENTS

To my mother, Venice, you are the first and most profound relationship in my life. The same love, respect, and infinite gratitude apply like always.

To Monifa Powell, thanks again for coming into my life. Thank you for being my best friend and my most trusted confidant and reader. I truly appreciate your encouragement throughout this entire journey.

To my inner family: Michelle, Jay, and Shanice. I love and appreciate you all. Special shout out to my two beautiful nieces, Summer and Autumn. I finally wrote a book you guys can read. To my father, Anthony Richards—Tony Brutus—Rest In Power. Live forever.

To Teneise Ellis thank you for being a friend and always taking the time to read my work. It means a lot to me. Bless you and your family. To my cousin Merrick, we are not only family, we are friends. Thank you always for your support.

To all of the beautiful people who have supported me and my many books throughout these twenty plus years, from A Hip Hop Story to Kali and the Black Tiger, I can not begin to express how much I appreciate you. You saved me.

A special thank you to my sister Judith. With out your support, I would not have been able to finish this book. You read the Arabian Nights to me as a child. I remember those nights fondly, and those stories have been a great inspiration throughout all of my work, especially this one.

To the Creator of All Things, I am forever striving to live up to the name you gave me. Thank you for giving me life, a dream and the ability to live it.